Book Description

The true face of injustice unmasks itself in this confounding book as we explore the cases of ten people who have been put on death row for crimes they did not commit. True stories of despair, fear, anguish and injustice that have become a permanent part of their lives even after being exonerated. Some of these people have lost their lives because of the poor investigations carried out by police. Some of these people have been a victim of circumstance while others were framed and set up for murders.

Corruption in the police department becomes more evident as each case unfolds. Falsified testimonies and evidence, racism and poor police work has sent countless people to prison and death row. Embark on this journey with me as we discover the events that led to the wrongful convictions and death sentences of these ten innocent people.

Falsely Convicted and Sentenced to Death

Ten Innocent People Who Were Put on Death Row

Paragon Publishing

Table of Contents

Introduction

As we dive deeper into the cases of these 10 innocent people who have been wrongly convicted of crimes they did not commit, it's also important to understand what played a huge role in setting them free from prison. Most of these people were convicted and sentenced to death during a time when forensic science was not advanced as it is today. There was no DNA testing done on evidence that had been collected from crime scenes, there was no proper fingerprint analysis done and evidence was always being misplaced or destroyed because there was no proper way of examining it.

DNA testing has revolutionized the criminal justice system over the past few years, and it has aided in proving the innocence of so many people who have been put behind bars, even those who have been wrongfully executed in the past few decades. DNA testing is so accurate and certain that it has become one of the major sources which is used to prove the guilt or innocence of people who have been indicted. This technology continues to grow each year and now there is a system profile that has been set up which stores data and information on people.

DNA plays a huge role in the release of many men who have been mentioned in this book. Clemente Aguirre-Jarquin, Jimmy Dennis, Clarence Brandley and Curtis McCarty are examples of men who have been released because of the breakthrough in DNA testing and forensic science. Men like Carlos DeLuna and Cameron Todd Willingham who were proven innocent after they had been executed. Let's take a closer look at each of these cases and explore the events which led to their convictions and ultimate executions and release.

Chapter 1: The Bridgeman Brothers: Wrongfully Convicted for a 1975 Shooting.

How the justice system failed Ronnie and Wiley Bridgeman, and Ricky Jackson

Three young African American men, Ricky Jackson, Wiley Bridgeman, and Ronnie Bridgeman, aka Kwame Ajamu, were wrongfully convicted of murder in 1975 in Cleveland, Ohio. They were sentenced to death; however, their sentences were commuted to life imprisonment in 1977. They spent decades behind bars before they were exonerated in 2014.

The Crime and Conviction

Who were they convicted of killing?

A businessman named Harold Franks was killed on May 19th, 1975, outside a grocery store where he regularly delivered money orders. It was alleged that three black men tortured and killed Harold; two of the men beat him up and threw acid in his face, then the other man shot him with a 38-caliber pistol. Anna Robinson, the wife of the store owner, was also targeted when they fired a round of bullets at her. They stole the briefcase which contained the money orders that were supposed to be delivered to the grocery store that morning, and they fled the scene in a green car driven by a third accomplice.

The charges brought against them

There were witnesses as young as 12-years-old who claimed they saw what happened. Eddie Vernon was the 12-year-old boy who claimed that Rickey, Wiley, and Ronnie were the 3 young black men who committed the crime. Although he was sitting in a school bus, he claimed that he saw these men's faces clearly. Then there was Karen Smith, a local teenage girl who saw two black men standing outside the store before the crime took place. Despite Karen knowing Ronnie, Wiley and Ricky, she testified at trial that she did not know the men whom she'd seen outside the grocery store that day. Apart from these two people, there were no other witnesses or any physical evidence against the three men. The briefcase that had been stolen, the gun and the green car were never found. This lack of evidence was clearly a reason for police to further investigate the crime and find some evidence that would be good enough to put these men behind bars.

These three men who were convicted of the murder were not your typical gangsters who roamed the streets looking for trouble. Ronnie and Wiley Bridgeman were described as "good boys" by their neighbors. They lived with their sister, their brother and their mother, Bessie Bridgeman. Wiley was in the Marines, but due to health reasons, he was honourably discharged from service. Ronnie went to trade school to become a machinist but couldn't find a job in that field, so he had to take up work somewhere else. The brothers never got into trouble and they were always busy with their own lives. Ricky Jackson was also someone who minded his own and stayed out of trouble with the law. Ricky and Ronnie were good friends.

Eddie Vernon's testimony led to the arrest of these three men. They stood trial and were convicted of the murder of Harold Franks, and they all were sentenced to death. Ricky was accused of being the man who shot Harold twice and he was never granted parole. Ronnie was accused of beating up Harold and throwing acid in his face, and Wiley was accused of being the driver of the getaway car. All of the accusations were based on Vernon's testimony. There was no physical evidence to pin any of these men to a particular crime. The prosecutors seemed to be content with putting these three men behind bars without proper evidence. And the lousy police work that was carried by the officers seemed good enough for the court.

Ricky Jackson was never granted parole because he was convicted as being the one who shot and killed Harold Frank. He served 39 years in prison and he was the only person in U.S history who was exonerated after spending that much time on death row. Ronnie spent 28 years in prison and he concentrated a lot on education while he was there. This proved to be a good choice, since he managed to land an office job when he was paroled in 2003. His brother Wiley was paroled in 2002 after spending 27 years in prison, but because of his mental health issues, which arose while he was in prison, he landed himself in trouble and was returned to prison for violating his parole.

Exoneration and Release

A man named Kyle Swenson conducted an investigation into the matter and published his report in the *Cleveland Scene* magazine. In his report there were findings which pointed to flaws in the case against all 3 men, and it questioned the 12-year-old Vernon's testimony. Then, in 2013, out of the blue, Vernon decided to recant his testimony. He was sick in the hospital and he confessed to a minister who had visited him. He told the minister that one of his friends had given him the names of the three men and he told police that he witnessed the crime.

Vernon signed an affidavit in 2014, stating that he was coerced by police to testify against Rick, Ronnie and

Wiley. He recanted his testimony and told police that he was not close enough to see the face of the murderers because he was riding in the school bus, which was a few blocks away from the crime scene. The Innocence Project had intervened and handled appeals for Ricky, Ronnie, and Wiley to help them get compensation for all the years they spent behind bars. On November 20, 2014, Wiley Bridgeman and Ricky Jackson were released from prison after a motion had been filed to dismiss the charges against them. Ronnie Bridgeman's conviction was also thrown out in December 2014.

Ricky Jackson was awarded $1 million dollars in compensation in 2015 by the state of Ohio for all the years he spent in prison. He spent decades serving time for a murder he didn't commit. Then, in 2016, Ricky received an additional $2.65 million dollars from the state Court of Claims for loss of income for all the years he was put away, being as he was the only person in the United States to have served three decades and then being exonerated. Ronnie and Wiley Bridgeman received a combined $1.6 million dollars in compensation for the time they spent in jail. They were later awarded $4.38 million dollars in compensation from the state.

In closing

An innocent man was beaten and killed over a briefcase filled with money outside a grocery store in Ohio. Three innocent black men were arrested and convicted of the murder. The arrests and convictions were based solely upon a teenage boy's testimony and on no other evidence. An investigation wasn't carried out to seek the real culprits, instead, the police had their minds set on these three innocent men and took them to trial. They were single-minded and they refused to investigate further.

The eyewitness testified that he had been paid money by the store owner who wanted him to testify in court. Vernon also claimed that the police told him if he didn't testify against these men, then they would charge his parents with perjury and throw them behind bars. Vernon didn't have a choice, so he testified against these men, sealing their fate with every word. The driving force behind the corrupt police work was a pure hate for African American men. This is how so many innocent people end up behind bars.

Chapter 2: Cameron Todd Willingham: "I didn't murder my kids!"

How the justice system failed Todd Willingham

Cameron Todd Willingham was convicted and executed for the murder of his 3 kids by arson on December 23 1992, when a fire broke out in the family home. He was executed in 2004. Texas fire marshals investigated the scene of the fire and determined that Todd had started the fire which killed his children. They claimed that there was some type of fire igniting fluid that was used to start the fire. Throughout the investigation, Todd remained steadfast and maintained his innocence.

The incidents surrounding the conviction

The devastating fire

It was an ordinary day in December, when eleven-year-old Buffie Barbee smelled smoke while playing outside. She ran inside the house and told her mother Diane. They lived just a few doors down from the Willingham's. As they ran up the street, they could hear the screams of a man who was standing outside of his house as it was being consumed by huge, red, fiery flames. The man was Cameron Todd Willingham; the man who was convicted of killing his three daughters. He was shouting "my babies are burning," crying out for someone to help him save his children, who were trapped inside of the burning house.

Todd was standing outside on the front porch without a shirt on, and he was barefoot. His wife was out shopping for Christmas at a local thrift store and the children stayed home with Todd. As he was shouting frantically, the fire continued to spread quickly around the house. When Dianne ran back home to call the fire department, Todd tried to break a few windows with a stick he found lying on the ground. Each window he broke, flames surged through it. Todd gave up and fell to the ground, crying.

Todd's three daughters, two-year-old Amber Louise Kuykendall and one-year old twins Kameron Marie Willingham and Karmen Dianne Willingham were inside their rooms when the fire broke out. Todd said he woke up in shock when he heard his daughter Amber calling out to him.

Firefighters rescued the girls, but it was too late. The twins were found severely burned on the floor of their bedroom and Amber was found in the master bedroom. All three children died of smoke inhalation. Todd sustained a few minor burns on his shoulders and his hair was scathed, but apart from that there were no other major injuries. Police were confused about Todd not sustaining any burns to his feet, this raised red flags for investigators.

The Investigation and the Trial of Todd Willingham

Later that night, after the fire, Todd was seen drinking at a local bar. The people of the town felt that his behavior was not on par with someone who had just lost their children to a fire. Police decided to carry out an investigation and on the 31st of December 1991, and the state fire marshal was brought in to investigate the home to find any evidence of arson. After corroborating his findings, the fire marshal declared that the fire was caused due to arson. He claimed that he found evidence of fire igniting substances being poured onto the floors in the home.

The investigators came to the conclusion that Todd Willingham had caused the deaths of his three children by arson. Todd's odd behavior and the fact that his feet were unscathed, gave police the impression that he started the fire from outside the home. Todd's wife Stacy described him as a loving father who spoiled his children often. He would never hurt his children, but he did hurt his wife, Stacy. Neighbors testified that Todd would beat Stacy on a daily basis. This raised even more red flags for the investigators.

Todd was arrested by police and taken into custody. He maintained that he was innocent and that he did not kill his children. At the trial, a man named Johnny Webb had testified against Todd. He was a jailhouse informant who testified that Todd confessed to killing his children because he tried to cover up an injury or death that his wife caused to one of his children. The girls had no sign of any physical injuries to their bodies, as confirmed after an autopsy was done. Jonny Webb's testimony was not credible, since he later told a reporter for *The New Yorker* that he could have made a mistake because he suffered from bipolar disorder and was taking a lot of medication at that time.

There were burns found on Amber's forehead and arms. Johnny explained that these burns were made with pieces of paper by Todd, to make it seem as if the children were playing with fire. The prosecutor could not find Webb as a reliable source as he sent a letter to the prosecutor, Johnny wanted to file a "Motion to Recant his Testimony." He stated that Todd was innocent and that he never confessed to killing his daughters. After some time, he then recanted his recantation. Such behavior looked highly suspicious for Johnny Webb. Despite what the prosecutor thought of John Jackson, the two had made a deal together; Jackson told Webb to testify against Todd in court, saying that he confessed to the murder of his daughters. In return, Jackson would find a way to release Webb from prison. Webb accepted the deal. Shortly after that, Webb was indeed released from prison. That fake testimony cost Todd his life and has tarnished his reputation.

A psychiatrist named James Gibson, who is well known for his death penalty recommendations, said that Todd fit the description of a sociopath because of his tattoo of a skull with a snake. He believed that it symbolized death and violence. He said that Todd was an incurable sociopath. Before his death, James was expelled from the APA (American Psychiatric Association) because he often diagnosed a patient without even taking the time to properly evaluate the individual. He did the same thing in Todd's case. It was unfair and unjust how these people in high positions treated those in lower positions.

At the trial, investigators testified that there were 3 points of origin for the fire. This indicated that the fire was set by Todd Willingham. They had found a piece of charred material near the doorway of the home. When investigators tested this material, it came back positive for containing a substance similar to lighter fluid. The investigators also mentioned that Todd's feet were not burned because he poured the accelerant around the house as he walked backwards out of the house. The prosecutor, John Jackson, commented that the first and second degree burns on Todd's arms were superficial, meaning that he caused the burns to himself to avoid becoming a suspect.

However, fire investigators who reviewed the case stated that the burns which Todd sustained were consistent with being caught in a fire just before flashover could occur. Todd was found guilty by the jury and was charged with murder on January 8, 1992. His abusive nature towards his wife, the change in behavior after the deaths of his daughters, and the testimony of Johnny Webb and the fire marshal's report all played a huge part in his conviction. He was offered to take a plea deal whereby he would plead guilty and serve life in prison instead of being executed. Todd turned down the plea deal, he could not accept punishment for a crime he did not commit. Especially the crime of killing his three daughters. He maintained his innocence until the end.

What was Todd's motive behind killing his children?

The prosecution believed that Todd Willingham had a motive to kill his children. They claimed that he didn't want the kids, and when his wife was pregnant, he would often beat her and kick her trying to cause a miscarriage. Although there weren't any police reports or medical reports to support this claim, the jury believed that Todd wanted his children dead. They made up reasons, arguing that Todd wanted to live a free life and he hated his kids. Stacy told prosecutors that Todd was an abusive husband, he would hit her every day and call her bad names, but he never abused his children. He was a loving father who cared about his girls very much.

As mentioned previously, Johnny Webb testified that Todd burnt his children to cover up a murder or injury that was caused by Stacy. However, this was untrue as the medical examiner didn't find any evidence of physical abuse on the children, and he determined that the cause of death was due to smoke inhalation, not from abuse. Everyone who was involved in the case felt that Todd wanted to kill his daughters, as he didn't want the burden of kids on his shoulders. However, Todd's former probation officer, Polly Goodwin, said that he never behaved out of the ordinary to indicate that he had sociopathic traits. She claimed that Todd could not have killed his children and that he was a good guy.

Later Findings

In 2004, a decade after Todd was convicted of killing his daughters, a team of nine nationally renowned experts reviewed the case for five years and found that the forensic reports and analysis were wrong. The Forensic Science Commission hired Craig Beyler to review the reports filed by the fire marshal. He determined that the "findings of arson" were not sustained, and the investigators did not follow the "standard of care" when investigating the fire. Each indicator which pointed to arson was not scientifically correct, and the investigators did not do a thorough search for any electrical faults. The piece of material that tested positive for lighter fluid was found outside the home near the barbeque grill on the front porch, which indicated it was used to clean the grill.

Gerald Hurst, a world-renowned fire expert, reported that the fire was not caused due to arson, but due to an electrical fault in the Christmas tree lights' wiring. The rapid spread of the fire was caused by the "flashover." A flashover occurs when the furniture in an ignited room reaches its autoignition temperature and then starts to emit flammable gasses which spread throughout the house. This was an explanation for why Todd's feet weren't burnt. The floor was not on fire when Todd was running out of the house. The fire was above, spreading on the walls and the roof of the home.

As for not being able to save his children, Todd carried that guilt with him until he died. He was too afraid of going back into the house. Gerald Hurst submitted his findings to the court just four days before the execution date. His attorneys filed for a stay of execution, but their reports were overlooked and ignored. The execution was carried out as planned and Todd died on February 17, 2004.

In closing

Cameron Todd Willingham was executed for a crime he did not commit. As a father, he loved his children and could not picture life without them. He always said that it was better for him to die and go spend eternity with his girls up in heaven than to serve life in prison without his daughters. The analysis and fire reports were based on assumptions from the fire marshall. The testimony provided by Todd's cellmate, Johnny Webb, was not reliable because of the repeated recantations to his testimony. The prosecutors based their opinions about him off the fact that he abused his wife.

The unfair judgements made on Todd by his neighbors, by the prosecutors and by the investigators led to his death. The investigation was not thorough because they already had made their minds up about Todd. They overlooked the new evidence and stuck with the old evidence that turned out to be 100% wrong. They already painted him out as the killer, so they chose not to carry on any further investigations before executing him. Now he has his wish, he is spending eternity with his daughters.

Chapter 3: Troy Davis: Executed for The Murder of a Police Officer

How the justice system failed Troy Davis

Troy Davis was convicted of shooting police officer Mark Mcphail on August 19, 1989, and he was sentenced to death and executed on September 21, 2011. He maintained his innocence right up until he was executed. Troy was a victim of "tunnel vision" by the police officers who were investigating the case. As soon as Troy was named a suspect in the murder, the police set their sights on Troy and were determined to convict him for the crime. They disregarded any new evidence that pointed the investigation away from Troy. An innocent man lost his life because of judgmental police officers.

The events that led up to Troy Davis's execution

The crime

There were three different events which took place on August 18, 1989. The events influenced the investigations on the murder of Mark Mcphail. Officer Mark Mcphail was married with two kids. He was a loving father to a two-year-old daughter and an infant son. He was just 27-years old at the time of his death. There was a pool party going on in Savannah, Georgia, on the day of the murder. Troy Davis was a coach at the Savannah police athletic league, and he signed up for the United States Marine Corps. He attended the pool party, which he later left with his friend, Darryl Collins. As the two were walking to a nearby pool hall, they noticed a car drive by, and the passengers in the car were shouting and swearing at a group of teenagers.

One of the enraged teenagers retaliated by opening fire at the occupants in the car. One of the passengers got shot in the jaw. The boys witnessed the shooting, and as frightened as they were, Troy and Darryl continued walking to the pool hall.

Troy and Darryl decided to go to a local Burger King that wasn't too far away from the pool hall. It was around 1:15 am on August 19,1989. There they noticed another fight taking place. This fight was between a homeless man, Larry Young, and another guy named Sylvester "Redd" Coles. They two men were arguing over alcohol. Young was pistol-whipped but could not identify his attacker. An off-duty police officer was working as a security guard at the Burger King when he noticed a fight break out in the parking lot.

Mark intervened in the fight, trying to prevent a dangerous situation from taking place. He was shot twice by the attacker. One bullet went through his heart and the other bullet went through his face. Despite the violent situation, officer Mark didn't draw his gun. Investigators retrieved bullets and shell casings from the crime scene that belonged to a 38-caliber pistol. The whole incident happened so fast, witnesses claimed that a man wearing a white shirt had pistol-whipped Young and then shot officer Mark. During the investigations, "Redd" identified Davis as the shooter, telling police that Davis was carrying a 38-caliber pistol. He also told police that the man who attacked Young was none other than Davis. "Redd" conveniently forgot to mention to police that he also owned a 38-caliber gun and had it with him on the night of the incident.

Troy Davis later drove to Atlanta with his sister on the same evening that the incident took place. Police searched his apartment, but couldn't locate the murder weapon. They spoke with members of his family, as they were concerned about Troy. On August 23, 1989, Troy returned to Savannah and handed himself over to police. When the police learned that "Redd" also owned a 38-caliber pistol, they asked to test the gun, but "Redd" told police that he lost his gun.

The trial

At the trial, there were seven witnesses who testified that they saw Troy shoot officer Mark in the parking lot of the Burger King. Another two witnesses testified that Troy confessed the murder to them. All in all, there were six people who testified for the defense and 32 people who testified for the prosecution. The murder weapon could not be found. The bullets that were found near the scene of the crime were sent for ballistics testing and the results matched the bullets to another shooting, which Troy was charged with.

Troy's friend Darryl Collins told police, on the night of August 19th, that Troy had shot at the passenger named Cooper, who was travelling in a car earlier that day. But when he was cross-examined at trial, Darryl Collins denied seeing Davis carry a gun or shooting at anyone. Most of the witnesses who accused Troy of being the killer, changed their stories during the trial. Troy's mother testified that he was at home, and afterwards he drove his sister to Atlanta at around 9pm that night. The witnesses who said they saw Troy shooting the officer could not be relied on. One woman claimed she saw Troy's face from her bedroom window, which was situated a couple miles away from the parking lot at Burger King. Not to mention that it was around 1 am in the morning, it would have been dark, as well. How could she be so sure that it was Troy who fought with the homeless man, and thereafter shot officer Mark?

On the 28th of August 1991, the jury spent two hours deliberating on Troy's crimes. They finally came to a conclusion, and they found Troy Davis guilty of murder, aggravated assault, possession of a fireman and obstruction of a police officer. Prosecutors wanted to impose the death penalty on Troy. He begged prosecutors for a second chance, he told them that he didn't commit this crime. After deliberating for seven hours, the jury found Troy guilty and sentenced him to death. Troy's defense team requested an appeal for the death penalty that was imposed on him. None of the courts granted an appeal for a new trial. Troy spent the next 20 years on death row. He was executed on September 21, 2011, by lethal injection.

Who killed officer Mark Mcphail?

"Redd," formerly known as Sylvester Cole, was the man who fought with Young in the parking lot near the Burger King. He was the man who pistol-whipped Young and shot officer Mark with his 38-caliber pistol. Despite receiving leads and tips which pointed towards "Redd" being the killer, police overlooked the information and continued to pursue Troy as the main suspect. The investigation was not thorough, nor was it fueled by the desire to find the man who killed officer Mark. Police didn't want to spend any more of their time and resources finding out the truth and catching the right person.

The same black man who accused Troy Davis of murdering police officer Mark Mcphail, was the same man who committed the crime with his own hands. He threw an innocent black man under the bus for a crime he committed. In the black community, there is a code which they all live by. No matter the circumstances, one black person would never snitch on another black person. But Sylvester Cole broke that code when he implicated Troy Davis. Even though the two men were not acquainted, they still shared the code of brothers in color.

The Struggle for Justice

Just months before the execution, seven out of nine witnesses who testified against Troy at the trial, had recanted their testimonies. The innocence project sent a letter to the Board of Pardons in Georgia to overturn Troy's execution penalty to life, since there were legitimate questions surrounding his guilt. There were people from all over the country who urged the state to place a stay on the execution. Politicians, celebrities, the NAACP, Amnesty International, and the Innocence Project, believed that Troy was innocent and pleaded with the courts. A total of 660,000 people signed a petition calling on the board of paroles to stay the execution. But the prosecutors turned a deaf ear to their pleas and executed Troy as planned. Their minds were set, and they disregarded any new evidence and findings in the case.

On the morning of the execution, Troy Davis wanted to share a message with the world. He requested that Wende-Gozan Brown share the message on his behalf. "The struggle for justice doesn't end with me. The struggle is for the Troy Davises who came before me and who will come after me," he said. Troy knew that the justice system wasn't going to change anytime soon. He knew that every black man would be a target for police officers. He knew that there would be many more Troy Davises who would be convicted of crimes that they did not commit or have any relation to.

Looking at Troy Davis's conviction, he spent 20 years of his life behind prison walls. He was then executed, after serving all of those years. Troy was innocent, and he maintained his innocence for 20 years. When someone is sentenced to death, they should be executed within the first two years of being convicted. Allowing them to sit on death row for 20 years and then executing them is a form of torture. The justice system has failed countless Americans who have trusted the courts to give them a fair trial. That is the reason why so many cases of domestic abuse, violence, and murders of black Americans aren't reported to the police. They know that the police can't help them get the justice they deserve.

In closing

Troy Davis was a victim of implication and "tunnel vision." Despite all the cracks that started to show in the investigation, police never investigated any new leads. The whole conviction and execution seems like a total set-up, and Troy was chosen as the man who would become the scapegoat for Sylvester "Redd" Cole and for the investigators who were looking into the murder. He would not be the last black man to be convicted of crimes they didn't commit. It was determined that last year, 52% of people who were on death row were black.

The death penalty is largely used on people of color, more so than on whites. A study was conducted in 2019, and the findings show that people who were convicted of killing whites were executed 17 times more than people who were convicted of killing blacks. This is appalling to say the least, the justice system is clearly operating on a racist level when convicting and sentencing black people.

Chapter 4: Jimmy Dennis: The Musician who Spent 25 Years on Death Row

How the justice system failed Jimmy Dennis

Jimmy Dennis, a Philadelphia musician, spent 25 years on death row for the murder of a 17-year-old girl named Chedell Williams. It was claimed that Jimmy shot and killed Chedell after attempting to steal her earrings. Despite being at the opposite side of town when the murder took place, Jimmy was implicated as the man who killed Chedell Williams, and he was sentenced to death by lethal injection.

The day of the murder

What Jimmy was up to that day?

It was the morning of October 22nd in 1991, when Jimmy and his father were having breakfast and discussing their favourite topic: music. Music was a huge part of Jimmy's family and it ran in his blood. Jimmy was part of a five-person group which was named Sensation. The group mostly played at local talent shows and Jimmy was the lead singer of the group. He always took pride in the way he dressed and his clothes were always neat and crisp. It started off as an ordinary day, Jimmy had to attend band practice that evening so he got dressed in blue jeans and a denim jacket and packed a bag of extra clothes to change into at rehearsals. Jimmy left home at around 1:45 pm with his father and he boarded a bus for the Abbotsford projects, his hometown where he grew up. His friend and bandmate James lived in the Abbotsford projects, and he was hosting band practice that night.

Jimmy had to speak to a few of the band members about some music material, so he headed over to James' house early. When Jimmy got off the bus half an hour later, not too far from Abbotsford homes, he was seen by Latanya Cason, a former neighbor. Jimmy waved to Latanya and carried on his way. Jimmy met a band member named Meredith, they stood outside and talked for 20 minutes. Afterwards, Jimmy headed over to Berkeley Street where his old friend Lawrence Merriweather lived. Jimmy walked past a line of buses which were parked at a nearby elementary school, and he waved at a few kids on his way, it was around 3pm already. Jimmy and some of his friends decided to go to a fast-food restaurant called Popeye's to get some food and then they went to a grocery store to buy some stuff.

After a while, Jimmy decided to change into a sweatpants and hoody which he carried along with him in his bag. He then made his way over to James' house for practice. Jimmy got into an argument with band member Charles Thompson because he arrived late for practice. The two fought frequently over silly little things, Charles wanted things to go his way, or nobody's way, and Jimmy could not agree with that. After practice, Charles left first while the rest of the band hung around for a while. They then walked over to a mini market down the street from James' house. There was a TV at the mini market, which aired the local news. Jimmy remembers hearing about a 17-year-old girl who was brutally murdered that afternoon. It was around 11 pm that night, Jimmy and his friends hung out for a little while more.

Chedell Ray Williams

The young teenager was shot and killed over a pair of earrings. They were not just ordinary earrings, but figure eight hoop earrings made of real gold. Chedell's mother would often worry about her wearing those earrings out in public, as she had been robbed previously at gunpoint for those same earrings. Her boyfriend had to pay a sum of $100 just to get them back for her. She loved those earrings dearly and treasured them. Being a young girl in high school, she loved dressing up and adorning her earrings.

On the day of the murder, Chedell and her best friend Zahra Howard took a bus after school to Fern Rock station. The station was in North Philadelphia, about a mile from Jimmy's father's home. As the two young girls walked down the station stairs, two men approached them. It was around 2pm when these two men came into contact with Chedell and her friend. One man was described as wearing a red sweat suit with white high-top shoes and a black jacket. He was holding a 32-caliber gun in his hands.

The men demanded that Chedell hand over the earrings to them immediately. Chedell and Zahra froze in terror at first but then after a few seconds they both started running out into the street. Zahra hid behind a fruit stand, but one of the men caught up with Chedell in the street. They ripped the earrings from her ears and when she tried to escape, they held a gun to her neck. They shot Chedell and ran off to a car that had been waiting for them. There were over a dozen people who witnessed the crime.

Jimmy's implication

A few months prior to the murder, Jimmy's solo career was taking off. He was working with Jewel-T, a rapper from Philly, and a local promoter, George Pratt, wanted to sign Jimmy to a label and a local record label wanted an audition from Sensation. Everything was falling into place and Jimmy felt as though he had the whole world on a string. Jimmy's life at home was improving as well. His girlfriend Helen was pregnant and he had been helping her raise her 3-year-old daughter. He refused to call her his stepdaughter and always referred to her as his oldest daughter. His second daughter was due in November and Jimmy was ecstatic to meet her.

Jimmy had no clue that he was about to be dragged into a murder conviction, sentencing him to death row. How could a man go from making beautiful music and raising a loving family to spending 25 years on death row? The city of Philly had been engulfed in murder cases, around 350 cases that year, to be precise. The murder of a teenage girl in broad daylight rocked the city hard and police were determined to find the killer. A few days after the murder, Jimmy's photo, from a previous misdemeanor conviction of drug possession, had been shown to witnesses during the investigation. Then the rumors began surfacing that Jimmy was the one who mercilessly shot and robbed Chedell Williams.

Jimmy and his dad decided to get his lawyer involved, and they called the police station looking for answers. Police told Jimmy that there wasn't any warrant out for his arrest and that he had been mistaken. The rumors, however, kept persisting. There was a group of people who named Jimmy as the killer out of pure jealousy of his music career, however, Jimmy was unaware of this at the time. He decided to go down to the police station to find out what was going on. Despite waiting for several hours, no one from the department wanted to talk to Jimmy and his father. Eventually an officer told Jimmy that there was no one by the name of James Dennis wanted for questioning.

On the morning of November 23rd, 1991, a detective showed up at Jimmy's door with a few other officers. It was around 8:30 am when they asked Jimmy to come down to the station for questioning. Santiago and Frank Jaztrzembski were the lead investigators on the case. They took Jimmy to a room for questioning. Jimmy knew that he was innocent, so he waived his right to a lawyer. Probably wasn't the smartest decision he made that day. He maintained his innocence and told police everything they wanted to know about what he did that day. As for the questions about the clothing, Jimmy told police that he didn't own a red sweat suit or a pair of white high-top sneakers.

Despite his cooperation with police, Jimmy was booked for murder that day and taken into custody by the investigators. They were so sure they got the killer, that they disregarded the lack of evidence needed to tie Jimmy to the murder. Rodger King, a top homicide officer, stated that the case was simple because the murder was motivated by greed. He claimed that Jimmy had no respect for life and that he premeditated the murder. Jimmy sat there in shock; he couldn't believe that this was happening to him. He watched witness after witness go up and testify against him. They all testified that they saw Jimmy murder Chedell with their own eyes.

Investigators claimed that they collected a pair of white sneakers, two black jackets and a pair of red sweatpants, but the evidence never made it to court, as the investigators claimed it had been lost. Jimmy's former neighbor Latanya, the girl he waved to when he got off the bus, couldn't remember the exact time she saw Jimmy that day. She placed him on the bus at around 4pm instead of 2pm. Band member Charles Thompson claimed that Jimmy had shown him a 32-caliber gun that night during band practice. It seemed as if all of a sudden, the whole world was against Jimmy Dennis. Jimmy Dennis was connected of the murder of Chedell Williams and sentenced to death. He was taken into custody and placed on death row where he spent 25 years of his life.

Life behind bars

Jimmy stopped singing the moment he entered the prison. He felt no connection to the one thing he embraced since childhood. In a dark, depressing place like jail, Jimmy could not connect with his music. As an emotional singer, Jimmy believed that if he couldn't feel it while singing, then the person listening wouldn't be able to feel it either. The amazing part about every morning in jail, he had a list of songs that would play in order in his mind. First song was "Trust in God" by the Winans, second was "Dear Lord" by John Coltrane, third was "Sailing" by Christopher Cross, fourth was "Glory days" by Bruce Springston, fifth was "If it's magic" by Stevie Wonder, and last was songs by Whitney Houston and Fleetwood Mac. These songs played in order to send out a message to Jimmy every morning.

Jimmy's life in prison was an absolute hell. He had the prison mates and the guards trying to kill him because of the inhumane murder of a young girl. While they all stood against Jimmy, there was one female guard who noticed him and realized that he was different from all the other inmates at the prison. She believed Jimmy was innocent, so she told Jimmy about an organization that helped her husband, who was wrongly convicted and imprisoned. The organization was Centurion Ministries, which was led by Jim McClowsky. Jimmy wrote him a letter asking for help, but Jim was overbooked.

Jimmy had to help himself. He was moved to another prison more than 3 hours away from his family. It would become even more difficult to raise his children from prison now that he was so far away. In 1994, there were a few people who educated Jimmy about the Law. Jimmy's family hired a local lawyer who specialized in appeals. They worked together to find cracks in the case. First, they found discrepancies with the description of the clothing, then with Latanya's testimony and then the biggest discovery was with Jimmy's band member, Charles. He was coerced into lying about the gun in his initial interview and then to repeat the lie at the trial due to pressure from the prosecutor.

Police officers in Philly were corrupt and racist and they had no regard for the truth. There were many officers who were arrested for their misconduct and racist behavior. Their abuse and racism were exposed to all, and people's eyes finally started opening. Jimmy went on to a pen pal website and wrote a post saying that he was innocent and he needed help. Tracy Lamourie and Dave Parkinson came across the post and were aware of the abuse that had been endured by young black people by the police. The two were activists for social justice and they decided to help Jimmy clear his name.

Once they reached out to Jimmy, he sent them an 18-page letter, which included documents and proof of his innocence. They created a webpage and uploaded all the proof and documentation related to the case. Jimmy was working hard with his team based in Canada. He was determined to get himself out of prison. He never gave up. He began to gain supporters from all around the world who believed in his innocence. Two years after Jimmy began working with his Canadian team, he was referred to Kathleen Behan. Behan worked as partner at Arnold and Porter, a firm in Washington, D.C who took on cases related to the death penalty pro bono.

Jimmy was very excited and happy. He felt that his hard work paid off. Behan assigned Jimmy's case to Amy Rohe and Ryan Guilds. They were junior associates who came fresh out of law school. Jimmy seemed more experienced and knowledgeable than they were because of him studying law from behind bars all these years. Jimmy developed a strong friendship with the two lawyers. Their investigations paid off as new evidence came to light. A string of faulty police work began to unravel. Police did not investigate the leads they received, and they withheld a list of potential suspects. On Halloween night in 1991, just one week after the murder, a man named Willam Frazier was serving time at a prison in Philly. He was on a three-way phone call with a friend and his aunt. His friend confessed to killing Chedell Williams along with two of his friends.

Frazier provided police with this information and even gave them the address details of the suspects. However, police conducted a lousy investigation and didn't find any of the men guilty. Meanwhile, Jimmy's dad died at the age of 80 while Jimmy was still in prison. This broke Jimmy, and he was very upset. He was determined to get out of prison and worked hard to gain the attention of anyone who could help. In 2013, finally a judge for the eastern district of Pennsylvania stated that Jimmy was not given a fair trial. There was important evidence kept from the trial that would have proved Jimmy's innocence. Jimmy was going to be set free after 25 years!

In closing

On the 13th of May, 2017, Jimmy was finally set free. The drive home was 6 hours long, so Jimmy prepared a playlist of all the songs that went through his mind every morning when he was in prison. Jimmy could now go back to being a father to his daughters. Although he missed so many years of their life, he was grateful to finally hold them in his arms again. Despite being released from prison, Jimmy missed out on many opportunities to make his dreams come true. He could have been a star today if it weren't for the wrongful conviction being slapped on him.

An innocent man who got through each day with the help of music. He believed that one day he would get out of that hell hole, but he didn't sit around and wait for someone to rescue him. He relied on himself, he believed in himself, and he did what he had to do to spark a motion in his case. There are so many men today who will just sit back and give up on their future, on the justice system, and most of these men have a lot of reasons to. But if they continue to stand firm and not give up, they can also spark a change in their lives.

Chapter 5: Clemente Aguirre-Jarquin: An Illegal Immigrant Placed on Death Row

How the justice system failed Clemente

Clemente Aguirre-Jarquin was convicted of killing 47-year-old Cheryl Williams and her mother, 68-year-old Carol Bareis 2004. He spent a decade on death row and 15 years in prison before being set free in 2018. He filed a lawsuit against the Seminole County Sheriff's office, due to their poor police work when investigating the case.

The murder of Cheryl Williams and Carol Bareis

What happened that night

Cheryl Williams and her mother, Carol Bareis, were found dead on the morning of June 17, 2004 in Altamonte Springs, Florida. The two women were found with multiple stab wounds to their body. Carol had suffered a stroke and was partially paralyzed. She was found on the floor next to her wheelchair, and she had been stabbed twice. Cheryl had been stabbed 129 times, which caused her to bleed to death. A man named Mark Van Sandt notified police about the murder at around 9pm when he went over to pick up some clothes for his girlfriend, Samantha Williams. She was Carol Bereis' granddaughter, and Cheryl Williams' daughter. She lived with her mother and grandmother but had spent the previous night at Mark's home and she left for work separately that morning.

When the police started their investigation, they found a 10-inch kitchen knife thrown between Cheryl and Carol's house and the residence next door at 117 Vagabond Way. The crime scene was covered in blood and investigators wondered who could have killed these two women in such a gruesome manner. When Samantha arrived on the scene, she told police that she had a very good idea as to who the killer was. She had a "gut feeling" that it was their neighbor, Clemente Aguirre-Jarquin, a 24-year-old man who was an illegal immigrant who lived with two other people at 117 Vagabond Way. He worked as a dishwasher and meal prep assistant at a restaurant.

Clemente entered into the United States illegally when he was running away from his home country, Honduras. There were drug traffickers who forced Clemente to join their gang and he had no desire to. He became terrified for his life, so he started running and never looked back. When investigators went to Clemente's home, which he shared with two other roommates, they had asked questions about the incident. The boys said that they knew nothing about it. Clemente went to the police after that and told them that he had been out drinking all night when he suddenly ran out of beer. The store was closed at that time, so he went next door to Carol and Cheryl's home to ask them if they had some beer to give to him.

Clemente said that he realized that the door was unlocked. This seemed odd because it was so early in the morning, and for someone to leave the door unlocked and go to bed seemed a little off. He then went into the house through the front door and saw Cheryl's dead body. Police arrested him because they felt that Clemente tampered with evidence that belonged to the crime scene. The knife that was found at the crime scene looked just like the knives that were used at the restaurant where Clemente worked. When investigators questioned the head chef at the restaurant, he told them that there was a 10-inch knife that was missing from the restaurant.

The evidence which was found by investigators was very compelling against Clemente. There were crime lab professionals who analyzed the evidence, there were physicians and police officers who also came in contact with the evidence. They all testified in court on the day of the trial. They found that Cheryl Williams had been wounded severely, and her lungs and legs were the areas that were targeted the most. The femoral artery had been severed and she sustained a fatal stab wound to her left lung, which caused her death. The numerous wounds on her hands indicated a struggle as they were defensive wounds, which meant Cheryl tried to fight off her killer. Carol had sustained a fatal stab wound to her left ventricle, which caused her death. But it seemed like Cheryl was the main target for the attacker.

The arrest and the evidence

Clemente Aguirre-Jarquin was indicted for first-degree murder and burglary on June 25, 2004. His trial took place in Seminole County Circuit Court in February 2006, almost two years after being arrested. According to testimonies from the crime lab professionals, the stab wounds were caused by the knife that was found between Cheryl's residence and the home which Clemente shared with roommates. The knife came back positive for blood which belonged to Cheryl, and Carol's blood was found on the blade of the same knife. The crime lab professional testified that Cheryl was killed first, and Carol was killed afterwards.

Investigators found 67 bloody shoe prints at the crime scene. 64 of those prints were consistent with Clemente's shoes. A search warrant was arranged, and police searched Clemente's home, where they found a plastic bag. Inside the bag were Clemente's socks, underwear, t-shirt, and a pair of shorts. The clothing was sent for testing, and it came back positive for Cheryl's blood on all of the clothing and on the soles of the shoes, and Carol's blood was found on his t-shirt, shorts, and underwear. Clemente's fingerprints were also found on the knife. This evidence told the story of what happened on that ominous night.

Samantha Williams took the stand and testified that Clemente had been a guest in their home many times but was banned from visiting again after she woke up one night and found him standing over her bed. Mark Van Sandt and Samantha testified that they both spent the night together when the murders took place. Clemente testified that he had a day off from work, so he drank throughout the day with his friends, which eventually got carried into the night. He then came home at 5am and went next door to borrow some beer from Carol and Cheryl and found them dead.

He then went on to testify that he picked up Cheryl's body and laid her onto his lap, trying to revive her, but it was too late. He then walked over into the living room, and that was where he found Carol. He saw the knife lying near Chery's body, so he picked it up and shouted "Is anyone here?" terrified that there might be someone hiding inside the house. There was no reply, so he went into Samantha's room to see if she was okay. He noticed that her room was ransacked, so he ran out of the house and threw the knife into the grass. He then took off his clothes and placed them into a plastic bag and showered. He was too afraid to contact the police and report the murders because he was an illegal immigrant in the United States.

Clemente was convicted of first-degree murder and burglary on the 28th of February, 2006. The Jury voted 7 to 5 for the death penalty for the murder of Cheryl

Williams and 9 to 3 for the death penalty for the murder of Carol Bareis. Clemente Aguirre-Jarquin was sentenced to death.

New findings and Clemente's release from prison

In 2007, Donna Birks, the fingerprint analyst who worked on the murder, came under review after her co-worker reported that Donna made a positive identification on a fingerprint that was impossible to read. Donna Birks was wrong when she said that the fingerprint belonged to Clemente-Aguirre. This led to a motion for a new trial being filed by Clemente, but it was denied. The Florida Supreme Court upheld all convictions and sentencing. In 2011, Clemente's attorneys approached the Innocence Project to ask for help in obtaining DNA testing for multiple pieces of evidence, 80 pieces to be exact.

During an evidentiary hearing in 2013, Clemente's DNA was excluded from the scene of the crime and Samantha's DNA was found at different locations at the scene which pointed to her being the killer. Clemente's legal team had also presented evidence to the court which proved that Samantha had a history of mental illness. She had been hospitalized around 60 times to be evaluated. She testified denying all claims that she was the killer.

She admitted to having a fight with her mother on the night of the murder. Mark Van Sandt testified that even though they went to bed together, he could not say for sure if Samantha had left during the night because he is a deep sleeper. Four people testified that Samantha confessed to them that she killed her mother and her grandmother. She said that demons made her kill them and she didn't really want to.

In October 2016, the Supreme Court ordered a new trial, and they vacated the convictions that were placed on Clemente. The new evidence that has come to light changes the focus of the trial entirely. After many different proceedings and trials, finally, on November 5th, 2018, all charges were dismissed by the prosecution. Clemente Aguirre-Jarquin was released from prison. In January 2019, his attorneys filed a petition asking a judge to declare Clemente a wrongly convicted person so that he could seek compensation from the state of Florida. However, the petition was dismissed because it was filed too late.

In closing

Clemente Aguirre-Jarquin lost precious years of his life, serving time for a crime he didn't commit. He was a victim of circumstance and he found himself in too deep. All of the evidence pointed to him, and he had no other way to prove his innocence. The lack of good investigative work on both the crime lab analysts and the police, led to an innocent man being put behind bars. They did not commit a thorough investigation and just went by the testimony of the actual killer Samantha Williams. Can you imagine how the real killer walks up to the police and pins the murder on an innocent man?

He always maintained his innocence, he tried to explain his side of the story to police but they had their minds made up already. When your mind is made up, no matter who says what, you will never be able to see the truth, and that is what happened in this case. Clemente's testimony made sense, it explained why there was blood on his clothing and why his fingerprints were on the knife. As compelling as the evidence was, investigators could have conducted the investigation properly before allowing an innocent man to take the fall.

Now that Clemente walks free, he has no home to go to, no money and no family to welcome him home. He has no life to go back home to. This is the reason why so many convicts return to jail once they have been released. They have nowhere to live, no job, nothing to start their lives with. So, they commit more crimes and end up straight back in prison where they have a place to sleep and food to eat. Clemente never allowed himself to go back to jail. He worked hard to get compensation from the state because he knew that's what he deserved.

Chapter 6: Carlos DeLuna: Executed for the murder of Wanda López

How the justice system failed Carlos DeLuna

Carlos DeLuna was sent to his death on the morning of December 8, 1989, when he was executed by lethal injection. He was convicted of killing 24-year-old Wanda López, who worked as an assistant at a local gas station in the neighborhood where Carlos lived. He was just 20 years old when he was arrested and taken into custody on February 4, 1983. Since the execution, there have been many doubts surrounding his conviction and investigations have opened again.

The crime Carlos was convicted of

The crime

It was a cold evening in Corpus Christi, Texas, on February 4, 1983, when a young woman named Wanda Lopez, a single mother, was found stabbed multiple times by someone with a buck knife. She worked at Shamrock gas station as an attendant, and during her shift, she noticed a person who looked suspicious enter the store, so she called 911. While she was on the call with them, Wanda was stabbed repeatedly by this suspicious-looking person, who was identified as Carlos DeLuna by eyewitnesses. Despite Wanda offering cash to her attacker, he still continued to stab her. The police could not understand why this individual would attack Wanda when she was being cooperative, offering him all of the cash in her till.

She kept saying that she was going to give him the money and anything else he wanted, yet he continued to stab her. It seemed as if the crime was not motivated by greed but by some other factor. There was no logical reason for why this person walked up to Wanda and stabbed her, intending to kill her, even though she was willing to let him take everything without putting up a fight or refusing his demands. Some would say that it was a personal quarrel between two lovers which led to Wanda's death, but Wanda didn't know the person who was stabbing her.

Confused eyewitnesses

There were several eyewitnesses in this case, but only a few of them saw what happened at the gas station that day. Kevan Baker was the first eyewitness to come forward. On that ominous day in February, Kevan stopped by the gas station to fill his truck up with gas, so he had to go to the office to ask the attendant to activate the pumps for him. As he walked up to the office, he noticed that there was a struggle between a man and a woman inside the store. The woman was the gas station attendant, Wanda López. He could not identify the person she was quarreling with. The man tried to drag Wanda by her hair to the back end of the store.

After realizing that he had been spotted, he left Wanda and bolted out of the store. On his way out, he came face to face with Kevan Baker. He stopped dead in his tracks and looked Kevan straight in the eye and said, "Don't mess with me, I have a gun." He then ran off towards the back of the gas station. The direction in which the killer ran could not be verified. Kevan Baker recalled that he saw the killer run towards the east of the store. This would become one of the major issues in the investigation because there were witnesses who claimed they had seen men running in different directions.

Shortly after the perpetrator escaped, Wanda staggered out of the store, crying for help. She eventually passed out and fell to the ground. Kevan ran into the store to get paper towels to try and help stop the bleeding and stabilize her until the paramedics came. Despite their best efforts, Wanda could not be saved. She died from her injuries. No one could understand how a crime so gruesome happened within a matter of seconds. It seemed as if the killer planned out the murder while he was standing outside the gas station that day. He went into the store with the intention of killing Wanda. Could it be due to her calling the police and complaining about him lurking in front of the store?

The next witness was George Aguire, he stopped at the Shamrock gas station at around 8 pm that night. He claimed he saw a man standing outside the gas station store. George Aguire was so confused over what he had seen the man dressed in. He described the man dressed in a long-sleeved t-shirt and a blue pair of jeans or a white shirt with rolled-up sleeves and black uniform-type pants. He said that DeLuna had been drinking beer and playing around with a knife. This made George nervous as he watched the man closely while filling his van up with gas. Suddenly, the man approached George and asked him if he would be able to give him a lift to the Casino Club, which was a local bar in the area. He told George that he would pay for the trip as he began opening a black wallet that had just a few bills inside.

Being as frightened and unsettled as George was, he declined to give him a ride to the bar. He knew somehow that this guy was trouble. He told Wanda to call the police because he could sense that the man was up to no good. As George got back in his van and proceeded to drive off, he saw the man walking into the store and a few seconds later the attack took place. He then drove to a nearby bowling alley where he asked the security guard to call the police. George later identified Carlos DeLuna as the man who committed the murder. There were two other eyewitnesses, John and Julie Arsuaga, who saw a man jogging towards the east while they were driving on the freeway. The man was Hispanic, and he wore a white shirt with the sleeves rolled up and dark-colored pants. They later identified DeLuna as the killer as well.

All these witnesses had different descriptions of the type of clothing the killer wore. Half of them saw him run to the rear of the gas station while the other half saw him running towards the east away from the gas station. Kevan reported that the killer had a beard that looked like it hadn't been shaved in 2 weeks, and the Arsuagas reported that the man they saw jogging was clean-shaven. It was clear that these witnesses were describing two different men. The police were confused because of the mixed-up descriptions that were being given by witnesses. The manhunt began and the police were after two men who fit the descriptions of the eyewitnesses. One was Carlos DeLuna, and the other suspect was Carlos Hernández. Two men who looked the same shared the same name, and they both were together on the day of the murder.

The arrest and the trial

After searching for 40 minutes, police eventually found DeLuna hiding underneath a parked truck. They immediately called off the search on the other suspect who was Carlos Hernández. DeLuna had no shoes or shirt on despite it being so cold. They found a black wallet on him with 2 one dollar bills inside and a clump of cash stashed inside of the front pockets of his pants. There was no blood found on him even though the crime scene was covered in blood. But he did have fresh fingernail scratches on his face and arms, and he looked like he hadn't shaved in a few days.

During the interrogation, DeLuna had mentioned to police that he was not the killer and that it was a man named Carlos Hernández. Police did their best to search for Carlos Hernández. They managed to find him and bring him in to be identified by DeLuna, however he could not identify Hernández from the mugshots. During a psych consult, Carlos told the doctors that he could not remember anything from the night he was arrested. After being thoroughly evaluated, he was found fit enough to withstand trial. There were two attorneys who were appointed to represent Carlos. One was Hector de Pena Jr and the other was Jimmy Lawrence. Jimmy was a more experienced criminal defense attorney and he handled most of the cross-examinations and he presented the closing arguments during the trial.

Carlos DeLuna took the stand in his own defense and testified that he was with Carlos Hernández on the day the murder was committed. The two had visited a bar called Wolfy's, which was located directly across the street from the Shamrock gas station. Hernández then headed over to the gas station. He told DeLuna that he wanted to get something from the store. DeLuna said that he ordered a beer and waited for Hernández to return, so he went outside to see what was taking him so long and that's when he saw Hernández attack Wanda. Terrified that people would think he was part of the murder, DeLuna started running. That was when the Arsuagas saw him jogging away from the gas station.

He said the money found in his pockets was from paychecks that were recently paid out to him. They then questioned him about his shirt, and Carlos explained how his shirt had got caught on a fence he was trying to jump over. Police had recovered a white shirt in one of the neighbor's front yard, it was later determined that it was not Deluna's. DeLuna admitted to the court that he could not identify Hernández when he was asked to by police. After four hours of deliberating, the jury found him guilty of capital murder. DeLuna had been jailed previously for two attempted rapes. After he was released from prison for the first rape charge, not even 2 days later, DeLuna had attempted to rape another woman. This proved to the jury that he was likely to reoffend if he was ever released from prison. So, they decided to sentence him to death.

"The Phantom" Carlos Hernández

Carlos Hernández was a man who was feared by his community. He was known for his bad temper and his criminal ways. Hernández had raped and killed multiple women and others were blamed for it. He treated women badly, and often raped and abused his former girlfriends. He had confessed to one of his lovers about how he raped and strangled a woman and carved an X on her back. Upon investigation, police had arrested one of the woman's former lovers for the murder. Hernández was not even considered a suspect. He would often brag about the bad things he had done to women and didn't really care who he told.

He bragged about murdering Wanda López and laughed at how the police had arrested his look-alike instead of him. The same knife that was used to carve the X on the woman he killed, was similar to the knife he used to stab Wanda. He felt as though he was invincible because he got away with so many murders, and he had good reason to think of himself in that way. The police never convicted him of any of the murders he committed. He was a vile human being who sat back and allowed an innocent man to be sentenced to death for his crimes. He died in prison in 1999, from Cirrhosis, while serving time for another crime he committed.

The justice system

The police knew who Carlos Hernández was. They had dealt with him in the past. The knife they collected in evidence from the X murder looked similar to the knife that was used in the stabbing of Wanda López. They missed crucial information and ignored several facts about the evidence, which indicates DeLuna was not the killer. But they overlooked these facts and convicted him of the murder. DeLuna also made it easy for the police to convict him because he could not identify Hernández during the mug shot lineup. There were no DNA analysis procedures being carried out on evidence during that time, so it made it difficult to catch the killer through scientific means.

In closing

Carlos DeLuna was crying out for help, he told police time and time again that he was innocent. He gave them valuable information on Hernández, which was ignored by the police. He didn't want to die for a crime he did not commit; he did not want to accept blame for a murder he was not responsible for. He was executed at midnight on the 8th of December, 1989 and he died with the stigma of being known as a killer. Before he died, DeLuna expressed his hopes that one day the truth would come out, and today it has, but it's too late. He has not yet received a formal pardon from the justice system.

An innocent man who lost his life for someone else's crime, he spent the last years of his life behind bars and didn't have a chance to live the life of a normal man. The justice system has left him in the past and moved on. As long as the world keeps spinning, life will go on. However, Carlos DeLuna deserves to be pardoned by the state for his wrongful conviction. He deserved to be heard, even after death.

Chapter 7: The Ford Heights Four: A Double Murder Conviction

How the justice system failed four innocent men

Verneal Jimerson, Dennis Williams, Kenneth Adams, and Willie Rainge, better known as The Ford Heights Four, were falsely accused of kidnapping and murdering Lawrence Linberg and Carol Schmal in Ford Heights, Illinois. Verneal Jimerson and Dennis Williams were convicted and sentenced to death. Kenneth Adams was sentenced to 75 years in prison and Willie Rainge was sentenced to life imprisonment. These four men spent over two decades in prison before being exonerated in 1996.

The events surrounding the crime and their exoneration

The murder and the initial trial

Lawrence Lionberg, a 28-year-old who worked at a local gas station in Homewood, Illinois, was kidnapped along with his 23-year-old girlfriend, Carol Schmal, on the 11th of May, 1978. Carol Schmal was raped repeatedly by the kidnappers and both Carol and Lawrence were shot execution style at the back of their heads. Two innocent people who were about to get married, ended up as victims of such a brutal murder that it sent shockwaves through the community.

There was a witness named Charles McCraney who claimed he had witnessed the events that took place. He claimed that Willie Rainge, Dennis Williams and Kenneth Adams were seen near the area where the crime took place in Ford Heights. There was a forensic state expert, Micheal Podlecki, who testified that one of the men who raped Carol, was a type A Secretor blood, which was rare, as only 25% of the population shared that type. Dennis Willians and Kenneth Adams were alleged to also share the type A Secretor blood, however, in 1987, an independent forensic expert witness found that Dennis Williams and Kenneth Adams actually had non-secretor blood. This was a red flag which indicated flaws in the investigation. Micheal Podlecki also claimed that he found Lawrence Lionberg's and Carol Schmal's hair at the back of

65

Dennis Williams car. Upon concluding their investigations, there was no other physical evidence found which could match these four men to the crime. When it comes to rape cases, usually DNA and fingerprints are gathered to find the rapists. Unfortunately, DNA and fingerprint science was not available at that time.

Red flags and Fake testimonies

There was a prison convict named David Jackson who testified that he had overheard Dennis Williams and Willie Rainge discussing the rape and the murder in jail. However, David Jackson later recanted his testimony and admitted that he was offered a deal by police, and he had to fabricate the story. Another red flag which pointed straight to corruption in the police department. And if that wasn't enough, the prosecution then eliminated every black person from the jury. The defendants were all black and the victims were white. This racial act from the prosecution was done to obtain the support of the white jury members in wrongfully convicting these men of the murders.

The police hid information from the defense team about a witness, Marvin Simpson. Marvin claimed that he heard gunshots and he had seen four men running away from the murder scene. He claimed that he saw these men and he was a suitable witness to place on the stand to help clear the names of the four men who were wrongfully convicted. However, the police did not bring forth this valuable piece of information, and they had their own motives for hiding the truth. The four men who were seen by Marvin were Arthur Robinson, Juan Rodriguez, Ira and Dennis Johnson. These four men were later proved to be the real murderers and rapists who killed Lawrence Lionberg and Carol Schmal.

The accused Willie, Dennis, Kenneth and Verneal, had an ineffective and hopeless lawyer named Archie B. Weston. He was in the process of a disciplinary hearing at the time of the trial, and he was disbarred from his position as a lawyer for another case he was working on. This poor work ethic and unprofessionalism from a lawyer, led to the case being fought by somebody who wasn't reliable or qualified enough. There was another witness named Paula Gray, who testified that she had seen these four men rape Carol Schmal and shoot the two thereafter. Paula had an IQ of 55, and she later withdrew her testimony and was then charged with perjury.

Appeals and reconvictions

The Illinois Supreme Court decided to reverse the convictions of Dennis Williams and Willie Rainge after an appeal was made in 1982. The reason for the reversal in the convictions was due to an incompetent lawyer that was appointed to the defendants during trial. A deal was offered to Paula Gray by prosecutors if she testified that she had seen Verneal Jimerson, Willie Rainge and Dennis Williams rape Carol Schmal and shoot both victims, then they would allow her to walk free out of jail, she gladly accepted the deal. In McCraney's initial testimony, he did not mention

Verneal Jimerson's name, however, in 1985, he changed his testimony and now included Verneal Jimerson in it. In 1987 Dennis Williams was sentenced to death, Willie Rainge was sentenced to life and Verneal Jimerson was sentenced to death. Paula Gray was released from prison in 1987.

Exoneration

Laura Sullivan, an award-winning investigative correspondent for the NPR, and three female students who worked under Professor David Protess of the Northwestern University Medill School of Journalism, had investigated the case. They found the statement made by Marvin Simpson about seeing Ira and Dennis Johnson, Rodríguez and Robinson running away from the crime scene, which police hid from the defense team. They also saw that Paula Gray and Jackson withdrew their testimonies. They were astonished at how such injustice had been done to these four innocent men.

The students decided to run some DNA tests which showed that Verneal Jimmerson, Willie Rainge, Dennis Williams and Kenneth Adams were innocent. By the time the real killers confessed to the murder and rape, one of them had already died, Dennis Johnson. However, Ira Johnson, Rodríguez, and Robinson had confessed to the crime and they were convicted. The Ford Heights Four, Willie Rainge, Dennis Williams, Kenneth Adams and Verneal Jimerson were exonerated and released from prison in 1996 after serving more than two decades behind bars.

The famous Ford Heights Four had been compensated with a lump sum amount of $36 million dollars in 1999, for civil rights damages from Cook County and it was the largest settlement paid out in US history during that time. In March of 2003, Dennis Williams died from a heart attack. He was only 46 years old when he died. The other 3 men went on to live their lives the best they could. Willie Rainge became an alcoholic because of the trauma he faced from being convicted of a crime he did not commit. If it weren't for the amazing work from the students and Laura Sullivan, these men would still be in jail today.

In closing

The conviction of these four innocent men led to them losing precious time which they can never get back. Apart from all the lost time, they have also lost the respect of the community and of their family members. For all these years, they have been labelled as rapists and murderers. They must have endured terrible hardships from other convicts in prison, and their names have been dragged through the dirt. Imagine living with the label which reads rapist and murderer hanging over your head all the time, not forgetting the fact that you are completely innocent.

These men have been targeted by the police for some reason and the entire investigation was run by corrupt officers who had their mind set on convicting these men for the rape and murders of Carol Schalm and Lawrence Lionberg. All of the red flags that presented themselves during the investigation and during the trial were completely overlooked by the court. From the reappointment of white jury members to the plea deal made with Paula Gray, the whole case screamed injustice, yet no one seemed to care enough. Being a black man in a white man's world proved to be the ultimate punishment for being born as a black man.

The so called "reliable" eyewitnesses who claimed to have seen Willie Rainge, Dennis Williams, Kenneth Adams and Verneal Jimerson commit the rape and murders, were actual liars who changed their testimonies when asked to by the police. How convenient it was for them to testify according to what the police thought was right instead of testifying what the truth actually was. Paula Gray sent four innocent men to death row just to get herself out of prison and she was quite content with that decision. Their conscience seems to have been turned off when they made these accusations against innocent people without any remorse.

If it wasn't for these students who took a stand to find out what the truth was, these men would have been executed by now. There is no amount of money that the state can award to these men that will ever bring back the priceless years they have lost with their family and friends. They lost out on a chance to build a life for themselves, to start a family, to wake up next to a woman they loved or to start a dream career. These are real life human beings that have been caged up like animals for years because of the poor investigation skills of the police department that went completely unnoticed and without fault.

Chapter 8: Earl Washington, Jr.: Convicted and Sentenced to Death Row for Rape and Murder

How the justice system failed Earl Washington, Jr.

Earl Washington Jr. had been wrongfully convicted for the murder and rape of Rebecca Lyn Williams in 1982 in Culpeper, Virginia. He was sentenced to death in 1984, but was later exonerated of all charges in 2000. A year after the crime occurred, Earl was arrested on unrelated charges and was then coerced by police to confess to a murder he did not commit: The murder of Rebecca Lyn Williams.

Earl was scheduled to be executed in September 1985, however, an appeal was made and a stay on the execution was ordered, while the defense team worked on gaining an appeal for his conviction. The defense team worked pro bono and fought for Earl because they knew that he was innocent. There were questions raised about Earl's conviction in 1993 and at the time there was no available DNA testing to help find answers to these questions, so Earl's death sentence was overturned to life imprisonment in 1994 by Governor Douglas Wilder. In 2000, DNA testing was finally done, and based on its finding, Earl was exonerated and released from prison.

The events that led up to Earl's conviction

The Rape and Murder of Rebecca Lyn Williams

Rebecca Lyn was a young mother of three children. She was brutally stabbed and raped in her home in Culpeper, Virginia in 1982. Rebecca was walking home from the store with her three kids that day. She lived in a gardened community and her home wasn't too far from the local green grocers. She and her kids went inside the house, leaving the front door open. Rebecca didn't have any reason to think that leaving the door opened would be dangerous for her and the children, since she lived in a very safe community. However, Rebecca could not have been more wrong. A man entered her home through the front door. He stabbed Rebecca a few times before taking her upstairs to the bedroom. He then proceeded to rape her. He stabbed her repeatedly after the rape and ran away. Rebecca managed to stumble outside, drawing the attention of her neighbors and a few police officers. With her last breath she described her attacker as a black man with a beard.

Earl Washington Jr., a mentally challenged black man, was arrested for breaking into a neighbor's home while under the influence of alcohol and wounding them during a disagreement. Police saw this as the perfect opportunity to frame Earl for the murder and rape of Rebecca Lyn Williams and another three charges based on sexual assaults. Earl confessed to the rape and murders without being in his full mental capacity. These three charges didn't stand for long and were disproven with the help of statements from witnesses and physical evidence. However, the murder and rape case stuck, and Earl went to trial because of the confession he made after police had rehearsed and reshaped it to make sense to Earl.

Coerced into a confession

During questioning, Earl made a lot of mistakes that were often corrected in a misleading way by the police officers. He agreed to the investigators' corrections, but he still managed to get the victim's race wrong, and he couldn't provide accurate details of the crime scene or about how he committed the crime. The confession was somehow good enough to send Earl to trial and to convict him of murder. The defense team did not represent Earl well at the trial. They managed to leave out the most important detail about him, and that was his intellectual disability. Everything was planned and everyone had a part to play in convicting the innocent man. Earl was sentenced to death for committing capital murder.

In 1985, a short while before Earl was scheduled to be executed, Joseph Giarratano, a fellow inmate on death row, took on Earl's case and noted his mental state of mind as being unstable. Joseph decided to contact a volunteer lawyer, Marie Deans, with whom he worked before. She took on cases pro bono and she helped inmates get a stay of execution. The defense team sent in a request to the court to conduct a DNA analysis of the evidence collected from the crime scene. The evidence showed that the semen stain was not made by Earl, which raised high doubts about the possibility that he was the murderer and rapist.

The Court of Appeals in Virginia had strict limits on when new evidence can be brought in after conviction, so they refused to hear the case. It was nine days before Earl was going to be executed when Governor Douglas Wilder commuted Earl's death sentence to life imprisonment. New DNA testing technology came about in 2000 that was more accurate. The tests connected another man to the crime and Earl was exonerated with a full pardon from Governor James Gilmore. Earl had a great defense team in front of him, Eric M. Freedman, Gerald Zerkin, Robert T. Hall and Barry A. Weinstein made up the team of lawyers who fought for him.

Compensation and the real killer found

Agent Curtis R. Wilmore awarded Earl Washington with $2.25 million from his estate because of the false confessions he coerced Earl into. In 2007, the state of Virginia and Wilmore's estate had come to an agreement to pay out $1.9 million to Earl for wrongful convictions from the state. In total, Earl was awarded over $3 million dollars for all the pain and suffering he experienced while he was in prison. A man named Kenneth Tinsley was serving a life sentence and he had been matched to the DNA found from the crime scene. He then plead guilty to the rape and murder or Rebecca Lyn Williams.

How has Earl Washington's case affected change?

Earl Washington's exoneration has convinced the United States Supreme Court that the death penalty should not be imposed on persons with an intellectual disability. The state ordered the review of all cases of people who were put on death row and who had some sort of mental illness or disability. Their sentences were commuted to the appropriate levels of punishment. This was a remarkable change that led to many lives being saved.

In closing

This was yet another case that had displayed the corrupt nature of police officers who implicate black men for crimes they did not commit. Earl Washington had nothing to do with the murder and rape of Rebecca Lyn Williams, yet he was punished with the harshest form of punishment, he was sentenced to death. Being a mentally challenged man in the black community must have been hard for Earl. He made the perfect target for police officers who were looking for someone to implicate for the murder and rape of a white woman.

Can you imagine the brazen mindset these officers had when they were brainwashing Earl into confessing to a crime he did not commit? It must have been especially hard for Earl in prison, being a mentally challenged man. He must have faced insults and abuse hurled at him on a daily basis. And he wouldn't have even fully understood why this was happening to him, all he knew was that he was sent to prison for breaking into the neighbor's home and starting a fight with them. When Earl was released from prison, he did a TV interview and when he was asked about why he confessed to the crimes, he simply said he doesn't know why he did that.

Earl's case helped the state to open their eyes and see that there is a big chance that people are wrongfully convicted of crimes every day because of their disabilities, or their race or their status. It all depends on who's investigating the case and they ultimately determine your fate.

Chapter 9: Clarence Brandley: Convicted of Raping and Murdering a 16-Year-Old Student

How the justice system failed Clarence Brandley

Clarence Brandley was wrongfully convicted in 1981 of raping and killing a 16-year-old high school girl named Cheryl Dee Fergeson. He was placed on death row, where he spent 9 years before being released in 1990. He faced many challenges upon his release, including child support payments and a lawsuit against the state that was unsuccessful.

The crime and its aftermath

The rape and murder of Cheryl Dee Fergeson

Clarence Brandley worked as a janitor at a high school in Conroe, Texas, when a 16-year-old girl was brutally raped and killed. The girl was Cheryl Dee Fergeson from Bellville, Texas. She was visiting the high school during a volleyball match which she was participating in that day. She went missing at the school and a few of her friends approached Clarence Brandley and Henry, enquiring about the whereabouts of Cheryl Dee. The two men offered to help find young Cheryl, so they began searching the school grounds.

Cheryl's body was found in a loft, above the auditorium, by Clarence Brandley and Henry Peace. She had been raped and murdered and her body was left there by the attacker. Immediately, Clarence and Henry became number one suspects because they were the ones who found the body. Henry Peace was a white man and Clarence Brandley was an African American man. The police took the two men to the station to be interrogated. Upon questioning the two men, Texas Ranger Wesley Styles made a statement that proved how corrupt and racist the law really was. He told the men that one of them was going to have to hang for the crime, and since Clarence Brandley was a black man, he would be the person chosen for execution. This speaks volumes against police brutality and corruption in America. Men of color are targets for police because they are looked down upon and treated as criminals despite being good and working hard. Clarence Brandley was targeted by police and the investigation took a turn.

The Investigation

Police questioned four co-workers, who were white, about the events that took place that day. Three of them said that they had seen Cheryl Dee go into the girls' restroom, which was located near the school gymnasium. A short while later, they saw Clarence Brandley walking towards the restroom. They notified him about a girl being inside the restroom, but he said he was going to put toilet paper in the boys' restroom. Henry Peace, the fourth co-worker, said that Clarence was adamant on searching the auditorium where the body was found. He said that Clarence calmly checked the girl for a pulse and thereafter notified the police. All four of the co-workers stated that Clarence was the only one who had the keys to the auditorium.

Clarence maintained his innocence throughout the entire investigation. On the 28th of August, 1980, a few days after the murder, Clarence stood before an all-white jury and professed his innocence. His testimony contradicted those statements made by his co-workers. However, he never went back on his word. He agreed that for 30 minutes he was nowhere to be seen because he was sitting in the custodian's office listening to music and smoking a cigarette. This was around the time of the murder. He also stated that he was not the only one to have keys to the auditorium, the other co-workers had access to it as well. It didn't take much to prop open the doors, anyway, stated Clarence.

Clarence Brandley goes to trial

Clarence Brandley went to trial in December 1980. The prosecution made sure that all black jurors were removed and replaced with all white jurors. The entire prosecution was made up of whites, and even the judge was white. The odds were being stacked up against Clarence and he felt in his heart that he had no chance of coming out of this now. The prosecution's entire case was based on evidence that was circumstantial. The witness statements from the co-workers were taken into account. There was not one spec of physical evidence against Clarence which pointed towards him committing the crime. Everything was based upon the hearsay of others.

The prosecution had stated that there was pubic hair found on the victim's body that was characterized as hair that belonged to a negro. However, the hair was never sent for expert testing and there were no testimonies from any forensic experts which stated that the hair belonged to Clarence Brandley. The hair was mysteriously "lost" from the evidence and has never been recovered. This places high doubts on the verification of the story about the pubic hairs. Other forms of physical evidence such as the sperm that had been recovered from the victim's body was never sent for testing and had been destroyed. Then there was the question of a spot of blood which was found on the clothing from the victim. The blood spot was tested and found that it was Type A, which could not have come from Clarence Brandley because he was Type O.

Out of all the white jury members, there was one man named William Shreck who believed that the evidence was insufficient to convict Clarence Brandley. He requested Judge Sam Robertson to declare a mistrial. His efforts were in vain. The public soon learned about William Shreck and how he stood up for Clarence Brandley. They became angry and started harassing him with phone calls. Police had been monitoring the communication made to William Schreck. They discovered that a man phoned him and told him that he was going to kill him.

As time went on, Clarence Brandley stood for a second trial in February, 1981. Despite the fact that there was a different judge, the jury remained an all- white jury. Not one black person took a stand to support another. The race card that the prosecution played to get the case swinging in their way was unfair and sickening. A man named John Sessum was one of the original witnesses who was supposed to be called by the prosecution during trial, however, he was left out by the prosecution because his statement did not match the other witness's statements.

Instead, the prosecution introduced a new witness who did not testify before. This witness was Danny Taylor, a junior student at the high school who also worked as a janitor for a brief time but was fired from that job shortly before the rape and murder took place. Danny Taylor stated that Clarence Brandley made a snide comment as a group of white female students walked past them, which was "If I got one of them alone, ain't no tellin' what I might do." This witness came up all of a sudden with a statement that made Clarence look even more guilty.

A medical examiner had testified that the victim died of strangulation by a belt. He claimed that Brandley wore a belt that was consistent with the ligature used in the murder. There were so many crazy claims that were made against Clarence Brandley, one being from District Attorney James Keeshan. He claimed that Clarence worked at a funeral home as well and that he must have been a necrophiliac, someone who raped dead bodies. He claimed that Clarence raped Cheryl Dee after he killed her. His claims were never proved to be true since Clarence was never involved in preparing bodies at the funeral home, he only ever did odd jobs around the place.

After the conviction

Clarence Brandley was convicted of the rape and murder of Cheryl Dee Ferguson. He was sentenced to death. New evidence came to light eleven months after his conviction; Clarence's lawyers found that exculpatory evidence had gone missing while in the custody of the prosecution. The hair that was found on the victim's body was Caucasian and did not match the victim or Clarence. There were photographs that went missing which were taken of Clarence on the day of the crime, and in those photos, he was not wearing a belt, as claimed by the prosecution. Even the sperm sample that had been collected was destroyed before the trail and this proved to be very troubling.

How could all this critical physical evidence disappear without ever making it to trial? There was no way that this was a coincidence, it was 100% planned and set up by the prosecution to frame Clarence Brandley as the rapist and murderer. Despite the suspicious disappearance of the evidence, the court refused an appeal and sustained the death sentence over Clarence Brandley.

A woman named Brenda Medina saw the broadcast on television about the Brandley case. She hadn't been aware of the case all of this while until she saw the television broadcast. She remembers her former boyfriend, with whom she lived, had told her he committed a crime that was similar to the one Clarence had been sent to death row for. The boyfriend, James Dexter Robinson, confessed that he raped and murdered a schoolgirl in 1980. He worked as a janitor at the school during 1980. Medina said that she didn't believe him at the time. She went to see the attorneys with her statement and after obtaining her sworn statement, Brandley's lawyers petitioned the court for an appeal.

The defense team also brought in a man named Edward Payne to testify at the trial. He was the father-in-law of Gary Acreman, a former janitor at the high school who had also testified against Clarence during the first trial. Edward Payne testified that Gary Acreman told him where the victims' clothes were hidden just two days before the police could find them. This pointed to Gary being an accomplice to the crime as well. The defense lawyers also called upon John Sessum, the witness who was supposed to testify at the first trial. John Sessum testified that he told the Texas Ranger that he had seen Gary Acerman follow Cheryl Dee Fergeson to the auditorium. He heard her scream, and he was warned by Acerman not to say anything to anyone. Despite telling the Ranger what he had seen, he was threatened with arrest if he told a story that was different from Acerman's.

A stay in execution and Clarence Brandley's release

The community rallied behind Clarence and came up with ways to help get him a new trial. Reverend Jew Don Boney raised $80,000 to help pay for further investigations on behalf of Brandley. A private investigator named McCloskey, managed to obtain a video of Acreman saying that Robinson was the man who killed Cheryl Dee Fergeson. He saw where Robinson hid her clothes in a dumpster and that was how he knew where they were. Brandley was scheduled to be executed in 6 days time when judge Coker granted a stay of execution.

The defense lawyers appealed for another evidentiary hearing. The Court of Criminal Appeals granted a new hearing. The hearing took place on the 30th of June, 1987 and Gary Acreman, Robinson and Texas Ranger Styles testified. Robinson admitted to telling his girlfriend that he was involved in the murder just to scare her because he didn't want to marry her, as she was pregnant. Acreman stuck to his story and placed Robinson at the high school that morning of the crime. Robinson and Acerman both had Type A blood, which matched the spot on the victim's clothing.

A new trial was granted to Clarence Brandley based on the new findings, which shocked the judge. He claimed that he had never seen such a corrupt case in his 30-year career. Clarence was proven innocent at the trial and was set free on October 1, 1990.

In closing

This heartbreaking case is the perfect example of how innocent black men are targeted and framed for heinous crimes. This case, however, was a cover up for a white criminal. The person who raped and murdered Cheryl Dee Ferguson, was a white male. The police department and the Texas Ranger Styles tried to cover up the action of a white man, by blaming a black man for the crime. He did everything in his power to make sure that Clarence Brandley went to prison for the crimes of another.

Justice did prevail for Clarence Brandley and he walked out of prison as a free man. Although he suffered very much at the hands of the justice system, Clarence wasn't even compensated for his wrongful convictions. He now lives his life as a simple man, trying to pick up the pieces and move on.

Chapter 10: Curtis McCarty: A Man Who Spent 21 Years on Death Row

How the justice system failed Curtis McCarty

Curtis McCarty was convicted of a murder he did not commit and was sentenced to death. He was convicted twice and sentenced to death three times due to misconduct from the prosecution and incorrect testimonies from forensic experts. He spent 21 years behind bars, including 19 years on death row. He was exonerated in 2007

The Crime and Conviction

What was the crime that sent Curtis McCarty to prison?

It was a regular day in Oklahoma City, on December 10, 1982, when an 18-year-old Pamela Kaye Willis was brutally murdered in her home. The cause of death was strangulation and she had been stabbed multiple times. When police found her, she was lying naked in her home. A regular teenager who lived a fairly normal life had been murdered in her home. The news sent shockwaves through the community and people were terrified that there might be a killer on the loose.

Curtis McCarty knew the victim, which ultimately made him a suspect in the case. Hair had been found at the crime scene and it was sent in for testing by investigators. The evidence was tested by forensic expert Gilchrist. She tried to match the hair from the crime scene with hair from the suspect, McCarty, but it came back as a negative match. McCarty had been questioned and interrogated by police for three years after the murder took place, but they never arrested him, he was arrested in 1985. Around the time Curtis was arrested, Gilchrist, the forensic analyst, secretly changed her findings. She now believed that the hair found at the crime scene could have matched Curtis' hair. Curtis McCarty's lawyers did not notice the change until the year 2000. During this time, Gilchrist had been under investigation due to her fraud in other cases.

The Trial

First Trial

The trial took place in 1986 and Gilchrist was supposed to be testifying against Curtis McCarty. She stated that the hairs found at the crime scene did in fact belong to Curtis McCarty. She had conducted further tests on the sperm sample collected from the crime scene and she stated that it matched Curtis McCarty's blood type. All the evidence had been tested by Gilchrist, whom we now know is a fraudster. Robert H. Macy, the District Attorney, presented the case very poorly to the jury. He committed misconduct by withholding very important key evidence from the trial which led to the conviction of McCarty. He was sentenced to death.

Second Trial

Curtis McCarty spent two years on death row before the high court overturned his conviction. This was due to the misconduct from the prosecution and poor forensic procedures and fraudulent comments made by Gilchrist on the stand. Because of this whole mishandled representation of the case, Cutis was given a retrial. In 1989 he stood for trial again with the hope that the truth would come out. Gilchrist would be testifying for the state again. She told the jury that the hairs from the crime scene could have come from Curtis McCarty. The jury was lied to yet again and the hopes of Curtis were destroyed. He was found guilty and convicted a second time and sentenced to death.

Third Trial

A new trial was awarded to Curtis McCarty in 1996, after an appellate court found problems with the jury instruction in the second trial. The trial lasted four days, and a new jury heard all the testimonies. They were also convinced that Curtis McCarty was guilty, so they sentenced him to death for the third time. Despite all of the discrepancies that were evident to the court, Curtis McCarty was still being found guilty and the death sentence was still hanging over his head. All hope was lost after that trial, and he felt as if he would never be able to prove his innocence.

Appeals and new developments

Gilchrist was under investigation for falsifying forensic reports in a few other cases apart from Curtis McCarty's. She had to re-examine the hair she collected from the Pamela Willis crime scene. She stated that the evidence would be suitable for DNA testing, however, she could not produce the evidence when the defense attorneys had asked her for it. She simply said that the evidence was lost or destroyed, and she had no idea where it could have gone. Up until now, the hair evidence has never been found, and some say that Gilchrist disposed of it herself to cover up for her fraudulent deeds. She was eventually fired after the investigation on her had been closed. Her false testimonies hadn't only ruined Curtis McCarty's life, but two other men were wrongfully convicted, Jeffery Todd and Robert Miller, because of the false testimonies she made against them.

In 2002, the defense attorneys were able to bring in DNA testing to Curtis McCarty's case. The sperm sample that was collected was tested for DNA and it came back negative for a match to Curtis. It was then that the Innocence Project took on the case and started to turn things around. They had consulted with attorneys Vicki Werneke and John Echols, who assisted with Curtis McCarty's case. A new trial was set in 2005, which finally proved that Curtis was innocent. The case was won by these attorneys and Judge Twyla Mason Gray ruled that the misconduct and fraudulent testimonies of Gilchrist had tainted Curtis McCarty's case and sent him to death row.

In 2007, there was more DNA testing done. Scraping from the victim's fingernails were recovered and sent in to be tested. The results showed that the DNA matched a male, but it was not Curtis McCarty. A bloody footprint that was found on the victim's body was not a match to Curtis and in May 2007, Judge Gray released Curtis McCarty from prison. He is the 15th person in the nation to be exonerated because of DNA testing and the third person in Oklahoma.

In closing

In this case, racism did not play a role in convicting an innocent man and sentencing him to death. The poor judgement and conduct of the forensic department and investigators are what led to this man being jailed for 21 years of his life. The justice system has failed yet another man. Investigations should have been carried out thoroughly, but it seems like once the investigators have their sights set on someone, they go after that person with all they have instead of putting that same effort into finding the real culprit. It's a pity that Curtis McCarty had to pay the price for their poor work.

Honorable Mentions

The life behind bars is nothing short of being in a hellhole, especially for the thousands of innocent people who were framed or set up for crimes that they did not commit. Since 1976, there have been over 1536 people who were executed, and it makes you wonder how many of those people were actually innocent. There may very well have been new evidence that had come up over the years which could have proved the innocence of some of these people who have been executed, but the courts don't really pay attention to the evidence once the convict is dead. Which means, they will never receive justice even after they've left this world.

There were a number of people who were executed by the state, but later strong evidence came up through confessions from the real culprits, DNA testing and other advancements in forensic science which proved their innocence. Here are a few honorable mentions:

Ruben Cantu - He was convicted in 1983 in Texas for allegedly shooting a man in an attempted robbery and was executed in 1989. He was just 17 years old when he was arrested. He maintained his innocence until he died.

Sedley Alley - He was convicted in 1987 in Tennessee for allegedly raping and murdering a woman and he was executed in 2006. Despite the inconsistencies in his trial, he was still sentenced to death.

Robert Pruett - He was convicted in 2002 in Texas for murder and he was executed in 2017. He always maintained his innocence claiming that he was framed.

Nathaniel Woods - He was convicted in 2005 in Alabama for allegedly murdering three police officers. He was executed in 2020 after spending 15 years on death row. He was set up for the murders because of racism.

Domineque Ray - He was convicted in 1999 in Alabama for allegedly raping and murdering a 15-year-old girl. He was executed in 2019. The day he was executed, the state didn't allow his imam to be present in the chambers with him. Only a Christian chaplain was present. He maintained his innocence until the day he died.

These are just a few men who have been mentioned among the thousands. The cruel and ignorant justice system has turned a blind eye towards these men and their pleas. Police corruption, improper investigative procedures, poor forensic work, and fraudulent testimonies have all resulted in sending these innocent people to their death chambers. Unfortunately, there hasn't been a change in the way police investigate cases today. There are still people of color who are being sent to prison for crimes they did not commit. No matter how loud their cries are, no one seems to hear them.

But there is hope in the advancement of forensic science and technology. With the help of CCTV cameras, smartphones, social media, and many other forms of modern technology, it makes it easier to find the real perpetrators today. The Innocence Project has helped save so many lives since their formation and they are working hard to continue proving the innocence of the people behind bars. Corruption and racism have to be eradicated from the justice system so that more innocent people aren't placed behind bars for crimes they did not commit.

References

10 Innocent People Who Were Sentenced To Death. (2014, November 13). TheRichest. https://www.therichest.com/rich-list/10-innocent-people-who-were-sentenced-to-death/#:~:text=%2010%20 Innocent%20 People%20Who%20Were%20Sentenced%20To

After 21 Years in Prison - including 16 on Death Row - Curtis McCarty is Exonerated Based on DNA Evidence. (2007, May 11). Innocence Project. https://innocenceproject.org/after-21-years-in-prison-including-16-on-death-row-curtis-mccarty-is-exonerated-based-on-dna-evidence/

Clemente Aguirre-Jarquin. (n.d.). Innocence Project. https://innocenceproject.org/cases/clemente-aguirre-jarquin/

ⓘ *The Ford Heights Four were formerly imprisoned convicts, who*. (n.d.). En.google-Info.org. Retrieved October 21, 2021, from https://en.google-info.org/51816809/1/the-ford-heights-four.html

Log into Facebook. (n.d.-a). Facebook., from https://www.facebook.com/NowThisReports/videos/583 593415463995/

Log into Facebook. (n.d.-b). Facebook. from https://www.facebook.com/watch/?v=12857454214856 65

says, J. W. (n.d.). *"The Phantom": The Unjust Execution of Carlos DeLuna.* Innocence Project. https://innocenceproject.org/the-phantom-the-killing-of-an-innocent-man/

search results - earl washington. (n.d.). Www.bing.com. from https://www.bing.com/search?q=earl+washington&cvid =f0f89b9dfb7a41edae68f8027764c9a3&aqs=edge..69i5 7j69i59j69i60j513j69i60l3.3497j0j4&FORM=ANAB01 &PC=NMTS

Troy Davis - Bing. (n.d.). Www.bing.com. 1, from https://www.bing.com/search?q=troy+davis&cvid=0620 415383844db994acfe2680852b48&aqs=edge.0.0l9.498 6j0j4&FORM=ANAB01&PC=NMTS

Printed in Great Britain
by Amazon

10454941R00056